¡Hola, Lola!

Lola and the New School

BY KEKA NOVALES

ILLUSTRATED BY GLORIA FÉLIX

PICTURE WINDOW BOOKS
a capstone imprint

Published by Picture Window Books, an imprint of Capstone.
1710 Roe Crest Drive, North Mankato, Minnesota 56003
capstonepub.com

Library of Congress Cataloging-in-Publication Data
Names: Novales, Keka, author. | Félix, Gloria, illustrator.
Title: Lola and the new school / by Keka Novales ; illustrated by
Gloria Felix.
Description: North Mankato, Minnesota : Picture Window Books, an
imprint of Capstone, [2023] | Series: ¡Hola, Lola! | Audience: Ages 5–7.
| Audience: Grades K–1. | Summary: Lola is anxious starting a new
school in the middle of the school year, but her grandmother's advice
helps her overcome her first day of school and adjust to the new school.
Identifiers: LCCN 2021047083 (print) | LCCN 2021047084 (ebook) |
ISBN 9781666337259 (hardcover) | ISBN 9781666343885 (paperback) |
ISBN 9781666343922 (pdf)
Subjects: LCSH: First day of school—Juvenile fiction. | Schools—
Juvenile fiction. | Grandparent and child—Juvenile fiction. |
Guatemalan Americans—Juvenile fiction. | CYAC: First day of school—
Fiction. | Schools—Fiction. | Grandparent and child—Fiction. |
Guatemalan Americans—Fiction.
Classification: LCC PZ7.1.N683 Lo 2023 (print) | LCC PZ7.1.N683
(ebook) | DDC [Fic]—dc23
LC record available at https://lccn.loc.gov/2021047083
LC ebook record available at https://lccn.loc.gov/2021047084

Design Elements: Shutterstock/g_tech, Shutterstock/Olgastocker

Designed by Kay Fraser

Printed and bound in the USA. 4882

TABLE OF CONTENTS

Meet Lola!

¡Hola, I'm Lola! I live in Texas with my family—Mama, Dad, and my baby sister, Mariana. The rest of my family, including my grandparents, live in Guatemala. That's where my parents are from. I know lots of interesting facts about the country.

Facts About Guatemala

- Guatemala is in Central America. It is about the size of the state of Tennessee.
- Guatemala has 37 volcanoes, but only three are active—that means they're erupting. The other 34 are asleep.
- The official language in Guatemala is Spanish.

Facts About Me

- I'm learning Spanish.
- I love history. I want to be an archaeologist when I grow up.
- I adore my family.
- I don't like change.
- I hate Mondays and onions, not to mention waking up early. Yuck!

My Family

Mama likes to speak Spanish at home. She is always trying to teach me about my roots and culture. Here are some other facts about Mama:

- She loves chocolate.
- She misses her family in Guatemala and wishes we saw them more often.
- She hates clutter!

Dad travels a lot for work. Since he is gone so much, our family time is extra special. Here are some other facts about Dad:

- He loves cars.
- He hates being late.
- He always makes us laugh!

Abuelita, my grandma, is one of my favorite people. She visits us once or twice a year. It is magical when we are together. She has the best stories. Here are some other facts about Abuelita:

- She cooks the best food and gives the best advice.
- She knows how to do just about anything.
- She is my favorite!

Abuelo, my grandpa, spends most of his time in Guatemala. (Don't tell anyone, but I think he is afraid of planes!) Here are some other facts about Abuelo:

- He loves Abuelita's cooking!
- He is always happy.
- He loves singing, telling jokes, and being playful.

Chapter 1

The Call

It was a call that started all the chaos. The principal at The Academy phoned to say a spot had opened up for me—starting in two weeks!

Mama was very excited. She had put me on the waitlist for The Academy way back in kindergarten. It was a lot like the school she had gone to growing up in Guatemala. I would have to wear a uniform.

Mama thought it would be a perfect fit. "Opportunity only knocks once, Lola," she said. "It's a great school. Going there will help you come out of your shell!"

I was confused. I was not a turtle or a bird. I didn't need to come out of any shells.

I was also sad. I liked my current school. I had been there for years. It felt like home. It had beautiful gardens, tall trees, green grass, and lots of green spaces. I loved my teachers and friends. I didn't want to say goodbye.

Everything would be so different at The Academy! I felt like a plant being yanked from its roots. I didn't want to change.

"Do I have to go?" I asked.

"You'll be fine, Lola," Mama said. She gave me a hug. "You'll still see your old friends."

I hoped she was right. But the only thing that made me feel okay was my grandma, Abuelita. When she heard I'd be switching schools in the middle of second grade, she booked a ticket from Guatemala to be there for me. She knew how much I hated change.

Abuelita arrived just before my big day. Dad went to pick her up at the airport.

"They're here!" I exclaimed when I heard the garage door opening.

A moment later, Abuelita walked in. She was carrying huge purse. My dad brought the rest of her suitcases.

"¡Hola, Lola!" Abuelita said, setting down her bag.

I ran to hug Abuelita. I closed my eyes as I squeezed her. I wanted to save this hug for a rainy day. With Abuelita here, I felt complete.

We sat down to dinner. Mama had made a special meal of tamales. I had even helped her bake a cake to celebrate Abuelita's visit.

I couldn't contain my smile while we ate. Abuelita was here!

"Do you want to help me unpack?" Abuelita asked after we'd finished.

"Yes!" I replied. Abuelita always brought me interesting treasures from Guatemala.

In her room, we opened her suitcase. It carried the sweet smell of flowers, coffee, and something else. It smelled like Guatemala.

"Where is it?" Abuelita asked, digging through her bag. But she couldn't seem to find what she was looking for.

Mama came in. "Time for bed, Lola."

"But what about my pres—" I started to protest.

Mama shook her head. "Tomorrow is a big day," she reminded me.

"I'll give it to you tomorrow," Abuelita promised.

I nodded and went to get ready for bed. After I'd brushed my teeth, Mama, Dad, and Abuelita came in to say goodnight. We said our prayers.

Dad gave me an extra hug for good luck since he was going on a business trip the next morning. He was going to be gone for a whole week.

I was nervous about the next day, but at least Abuelita was here now. Everything was better when she was around.

Chapter 2

Little Mirror

The next morning, Mama woke me up early. "Good morning, sunshine!" she said as she opened the purple curtains in my room. "Second grade, here we go again!"

Mama gave me a kiss and left the room. I could hear Mariana crying for her bottle.

I dragged my feet getting out of bed. Then I stared at the uniform Mama had set out for me. It looked huge. Mama had bought it big so it could grow with me. Wearing it made me feel like I was inside a circus tent.

What if the other kids make fun of me? I thought.

I was scared. No, I was terrified! I ran through a list of worries in my head:

1. I don't know anyone.

2. I don't know where my classroom is.

3. I don't know my teacher.

4. I don't know what to do if I need to go to the bathroom.

5. I'll be riding the bus for the first time—scary!

When Mama came back to check on me, I still wasn't ready.

"Hurry up, Lola," she said. "You don't want to be late!"

I looked at my uniform again. "I don't want to look like everyone else. Can I please wear my lucky bows?" I asked.

"That's a great idea!" Mama said. She made me two pigtails and put on two big red bows. I could smell her sweet perfume. "Now let's get downstairs before you miss the bus."

In the kitchen, Abuelita was preparing breakfast. She greeted me with a kiss and a big cup of hot chocolate! She knew how to sweeten my day.

"Buenos días, Lola!" Abuelita said.
"Come with me. I have a surprise for you."

I followed Abuelita to her room. She handed me a little box. Inside was a small, silver mirror. It was round and heavy, with tiny roses all around.

"My abuelita gave me this mirror when I was your age," Abuelita told me. "Now that you are old enough, I want you to have it."

I smiled proudly. I was honored to have Abuelita's mirror.

"You see the little roses?" Abuelita said. "Roses are beautiful, but they have thorns. Life is like that! It is beautiful, but there can be challenges, like starting a new school."

She paused. "What else do you see?"

I stared at my reflection. "I see myself!" I exclaimed.

Abuelita smiled at me. "I want you to see yourself as I do—strong, smart, and confident. Use it to remind you that you are loved and

that you can do anything. Not only today but
every day, Lola."

"Thank you!" I said. I couldn't stop smiling.

"Remember to take good care of your
mirror. You don't want to break it and have
seven years of bad luck," Abuelita warned.

"Don't worry, Abuelita. I'll keep it safe,"
I promised.

"I know you will," Abuelita said. "And I
know change can be hard. But if a spot opened

for you at this new school, then that is where you're supposed to be. Everything happens for a reason, even when it feels like thorns," she said with a wink.

I hugged her. Sometimes a hug could say more than a thousand words.

Mama came to get me. It was time to catch the bus.

"I am so proud of you! You are so brave, Lola!" Mama told me.

I blew kisses to Abuelita on my way out the door.

"Pay attention today," said Abuelita. "I want to hear everything about your day when you come home!"

I saw Abuelita grab her rosary, light a white candle, and start praying. I knew it was for me—Abuelita knew I needed all the help I could get.

Chapter 3

A Hug for a Rainy Day

As Mama and I walked to the bus stop, I repeated Abuelita's words to myself. *You are loved, and you can do anything.* But I was still nervous.

"Think of this like an adventure, a chance to explore a new world," Mama said. "You can do this!" She hugged me.

I wasn't so sure about that, but it was too late. The big yellow bus stopped in front of me with a loud *screech!*

I gave Mama a final hug, then picked up my backpack and lunch box. I climbed the steps onto the bus.

I moved toward an empty seat at the back, where most of the other kids were. But before I sat down, the bus started moving. I almost fell on top of one of the older kids.

"Watch it!" he hollered.

I blushed. No one had told me the bus would be this intense. I sat down quietly.

I thought about the mirror Abuelita had given me. I closed my eyes for a second and imagined her by my side. I remembered the hug I had saved for a rainy day. If she believed I could do anything, I could do this.

At the next stop, a big kid got on the bus. He walked right up to me.

"You're in my seat!" he exclaimed.

"Sorry," I apologized. I moved to another seat, but he followed me.

"That one is taken too," he said.

I didn't know what to do. Finally, I saw an empty row closer to the front and hurried there. I could hear the other kids laughing.

I slouched down in my new seat. I was ready to go home. I would beg Mama to take me back to my old school, where I loved my teachers and friends.

I wanted to return to my perfect world where I didn't have to ride the bus. Based on how things were going so far, this new school was *not* a good fit for me.

Two stops after mine, a girl with brown hair and glasses got on. She was wearing a beautiful blue bow in her hair.

The girl smiled and sat down next to me. "Hi," she said. "My name is Joy. I love your bows!"

I smiled back. I liked her already.

"I'm Lola!" I replied. I pointed at the bow in her hair. "Blue is my favorite color!"

"Are you new?" Joy asked.

I nodded. "Today is my first day."

"Well, I'm glad you are here!" Joy exclaimed.

Joy and I talked all the way to school. I asked all sorts of questions about The Academy. I learned that Joy was also in second grade, but she was not in my class.

Then I told her what had happened with the kid at the back of the bus.

"That's Mason," Joy said, looking in his direction. "Just ignore him."

I nodded, but I worried silently. *Is he going to do that every day?*

Chapter 4

A Giant Maze

Before long, we pulled up to school. My old school was small and colorful. This new school was big and gray. There were no green spaces. Just buildings on top of each other. It looked like a giant maze.

When the bus stopped, all the kids rushed off. It seemed like everyone knew what to do except me.

I felt the other students' eyes on me. They probably knew I was the new kid. My big red bows weren't helping.

For a second, I wanted to take them out of my hair. I didn't want to stand out anymore. But my bows smelled like Mama's perfume— sweet roses—and made me feel safe.

Suddenly, I felt someone tapping my shoulder. It was Joy.

"You seem lost!" Joy giggled. "Follow me. I'll show you where you need to go!"

I followed Joy to the gym. Music was playing, and there were kids everywhere.

"When you hear the whistle, you have to line up here." Joy pointed out a red cone that read *Second Grade B* in bold letters.

I nodded, trying to keep up.

Just then, a whistle sounded. Joy waved and went with her class.

I lined up where Joy had shown me. I repeated Abuelita's words to myself. *You are brave, and you are loved!*

But I felt overwhelmed. I fought back tears. I could not cry in front of the entire school. That would be even more embarrassing.

A lady with gray hair and blue eyes came up to me. She smiled kindly.

"Hello," she said. "You must be Lola Lopes Cruz. I'm Mrs. Bird, your teacher. Welcome to The Academy!"

I smiled. "Hi!" I said. "Just call me Lola!"

Mrs. Bird led me to my classroom. On the way she showed me where the restroom, the cafeteria, and the library were.

When we got into the classroom, I saw the walls were painted blue. They matched how I felt inside.

"Class, this is Lola," Mrs. Bird said once everyone was in their seats. "Today is her first day. Please make her feel welcome."

I was about to take a seat too, but Mrs. Bird wasn't finished.

"Why don't you stand up front and tell us something about yourself, Lola," she suggested.

My heart was pounding so fast that no words came out. I did *not* like talking in front of people. I couldn't move, let alone speak.

Mrs. Bird saw my face and seemed to understand. "Or maybe we can do it later this week," she said with a smile.

I nodded and sat in the only empty seat, right next to the door. Then Mrs. Bird started talking about my favorite subject—history!

Abuelita was always telling me about the history of Guatemala. Some of her stories were about people called Maya. They built great civilizations and knew a lot about math and the stars. Others were scary stories and legends about creatures like el Sombrerón and La Llorona.

So far, my first day was scarier than all Abuelita's stories combined!

Finally, the bell rang for lunch. My class went to the cafeteria. It was noisy and smelled a little weird.

I found a spot in the corner to eat. A girl came and sat next to me. I recognized her from my class.

"Hi," she said. "I'm Sophia. What do you have for lunch?"

I didn't say anything. I was too busy feeling anxious about what might be waiting for me inside my lunch box. When Abuelita was visiting, she sometimes packed my lunch as a special treat.

I loved Abuelita's cooking, especially her tamales and refried beans. They were delicious! But today, I didn't want anything that would make me stand out.

Please let Mama have packed my lunch today, I thought.

"Hello?" Sophia said. "Why are you being so shy? I just want to talk to you."

I got a horrible tummy ache. I couldn't answer. I was terrified of what Sophia might say if my lunch looked or smelled different.

I opened my lunch box and peeked in fast.
There was a note waiting for me.

I am so proud of you. Always remember to smile!
Te amo, Mama

I smiled. Even if things were so different
at school, nothing had changed at home.
I felt better knowing that.

Sophia huffed, seeming mad. "I'm just
trying to be your friend, you know," she said.
She got up and went to sit at another table.

I wasn't sure what had just happened. Did
Sophia really want to be my friend? And had
I just ruined it?

Chapter 5

Abuelita's Advice

The rest of the day went by fast.

After school, Mama was waiting for me out front. "How was your first day?" she asked as we walked to the car.

I thought for a moment. "Good and bad. The bus was scary. This boy named Mason told me I was in his seat, and I had to move."

"Maybe he was just having a tough morning. It was your first time on the bus, and you did it! Don't worry so much about a seat," Mama replied. She patted my back. "What was the good part?"

"I made a new friend," I said. "Her name is Joy. And my teacher, Mrs. Bird, was nice. She showed me around the school."

"That's great news, mija!" Mama said. "You're settling in already."

I sighed. I wanted to tell Mama that I missed my old school. But she seemed excited, so I didn't say anything.

We got home, and Mama went to change Mariana's diaper. I left my backpack at the front door and went to find Abuelita.

She was in the living room with a pitcher of freshly squeezed limeade—no ice. Abuelita didn't like ice. She thought it was bad for digestion. She always said it was like pouring cold water on a hot engine.

Abuelita hugged me. "How was your day?" she asked.

I told Abuelita about meeting Joy. I wanted to tell her about Mason and the bus, but I didn't want her to worry.

Instead, I told her what had happened with Sophia.

"She tried to talk to me, but I was so nervous that I didn't say anything. She got mad at me," I finished with a sigh.

"Don't close yourself off to new things," Abuelita told me. "Be sincere and kind. You get back what you give. With time, people will see how amazing you are!"

"Do you really think so?" I asked. "What if I never make friends?"

Abuelita hugged me. "Tomorrow you have the chance to write a new chapter. Remember what I said about the roses on my mirror? Once you move past the thorns, you'll find the beauty in this challenge. I know change is hard, but give this new school a chance."

"I will try my best, Abuelita!" I promised.

Mama came in with Mariana in her arms. "Lola, before I forget, tomorrow you'll be taking the bus home too," she told me.

I frowned. Taking the bus in the morning was bad enough. I had to take it home too?

Abuelita saw my face and knew something was wrong. "Are you okay, Lola?" she asked.

"A boy bullied me on the bus today," I confessed. "He made me move seats. He's scarier than your legends, Abuelita!"

"¡Santo Cielo!" Abuelita exclaimed. "A bus bully does sound scary. But you must remember that there are two sides to every story. Never jump to conclusions."

I nodded. Abuelita was usually right.

Abuelita smiled. "If it keeps happening, make sure to tell your teacher. In the meantime, how about a treat to turn your frown upside down?"

We went to the dining room. Abuelita took out a box of Guatemalan candy. I didn't see my favorite, *canillitas de leche*. They were tasty treats made with powdered sugar and milk.

"Sorry, I thought the box had them. Next time, I'll bring you a whole box of canillitas de leche!" Abuelita promised.

"Thank you, Abuelita! I'm just happy you are here." I smiled.

Abuelita set the box down on the table. "Try something else. Maybe you will find something new," she encouraged me.

"What if I don't like it?" I asked.

Abuelita smiled. "Have courage and be brave. What is the worst that could happen?"

I took a round, purple candy covered with sugar.

"Excellent choice! That is a *colocho*, a candy curl made of guava and sugar. They are my favorite!" Abuelita said.

Abuelita was right. I had nothing to lose. I took a small bite as Mama and Abuelita watched.

"And?" Mama asked.

"I love it!" I bounced up and down with joy. Abuelita was right. I had to be brave.

Chapter 6

Secret Garden

The next morning, I rode the bus again. This time, I made sure *not* to sit in either of Mason's seats. Instead, I sat at the front and waited for Joy.

When Mason got on, he stared at me. I thought he was going to say something, but the bus driver gave him a look. Mason rolled his eyes and headed toward the back of the bus. I breathed a sigh of relief.

"I saved you a seat!" I said when I saw Joy.

"Thanks!" Joy replied.

"Where were you yesterday at recess?" I asked.

"I had to go to the dentist." Joy smiled to show me her teeth.

Her smile was contagious. It made me smile too! Today was going to be a better day.

When I saw my classmates at school, I smiled at them. I discovered something: Smiling at people made it almost impossible for them not to smile back.

When it was time for recess, everyone ran outside. I noticed a big area covered by a metal roof. I was curious and went to look.

The covered area hid a garden filled with incredible rocks! There were red rocks, black rocks, and white rocks. They reminded me of the stories Abuelita told me about Maya ruins in Guatemala.

Who knew? Maybe I would discover a new civilization right here at my school!

I looked around and spotted Joy. Maybe she would like it too.

I hurried over to her. "Joy! I found a place with treasure. Do you want to come with me?" I was so excited to share my discovery.

"Let's go!" Joy said with a big smile.

We skipped together to the garden. We found flowers and rocks. We saw a cup and used it to dig and find more treasure.

"This is my favorite place to hang out!" said Joy. "It's like a secret garden."

I grinned at her. For a moment, I forgot that I was the new kid. I was happy!

"I'm so glad I came to this school!" I said.

"Me too," Joy said. "I have an idea. Let's make the tallest mountain ever!"

"Let's do it!" I agreed. We could build whatever we wanted in our secret garden.

Joy and I got busy making a mountain with rocks and decorating it with wildflowers. Then Sophia found us.

"What are you two doing?" Sophia asked.

"Building!" Joy said as she continued piling rocks.

"Are you ever going to talk to me, Lola?" Sophia asked.

I remembered Abuelita's advice: *You get back what you give.* Today was my chance to write a new chapter.

"I'm sorry I was so quiet yesterday," I told Sophia. "I was nervous. Everything here is so different. I was worried you were going to make fun of me."

Sophia looked surprised. "I just want to know more about you," she said.

I smiled. "Well, I love discovering new things. I want to be an archaeologist when I grow up. Then I can explore Guatemala! That's where my family is from."

"That's so cool," Sophia said.

"Do you want to build with us?" I asked.

"Definitely!" Sophia said.

I showed Sophia my favorite buildings so far. She started building with us. We were on a mission to create the most fantastic city!

"We can use my water to create a lake!" I said.

"We can make mud!" Sophia exclaimed.

"Yuck!" Joy shrieked. "Mud!"

We all laughed. We had to stop building
when the bell rang. It was time to go inside.

"Let's play together tomorrow too!" Sophia
said as we went back to class.

I smiled and nodded. I wanted to shout
with joy. Abuelita's advice had worked!

Chapter 7

Brave and Kind

The rest of the day zoomed by. Before I knew it, it was time to go home. Mrs. Bird called for bus riders to line up in the hallway.

I lined up with the other kids. When I got on the bus, I picked a seat in the front. Maybe if I stayed close to where I sat in the morning, I'd be safe from Mason. He had already claimed a seat in the back of the bus.

I saved the spot next to me for Joy. The bus slowly started to fill up. Joy wasn't there, though, and it was almost time to leave.

The bus driver started to close the door. Then, from outside, someone shouted. "Wait!"

The bus driver opened the door again. Joy rushed up the steps.

"Sorry!" she said. "So sorry!"

"Take a seat and let's roll," the driver replied.

Joy spotted me and hurried over. "Phew! Made it!" she said, sitting down and catching her breath.

"What happened?" I asked.

"The bell didn't ring in art class," Joy explained. "When the teacher saw her watch, she realized we were late. I had to run!"

I smiled. "I'm glad you made it!"

Joy looked toward the back of the bus. "Mason is staring at us," she whispered.

I looked too. Joy was right. Mason was staring right back at me. I remembered what Abuelita had told me.

"My abuelita says there are two sides to every story," I told Joy. "Look at Mason. He is always by himself. I don't think he has any friends."

"Because we're all scared of him!" Joy said.

Just then, Mason stomped down the aisle. He stopped right in front of us and glared. Joy shivered.

It was a little scary, but I reminded myself that Abuelita had taught me many lessons. Giving things a chance, for one. Like with the box of candy. I had found a new favorite treat. Maybe a chance was all Mason needed.

"Hi, Mason!" I said with a smile. "I'm Lola. I'm new to the school. I thought maybe we could be friends!"

"Are you kidding me?" Mason asked.

I was confused. "Why?"

"No one wants to be my friend! And I don't want to be friends with a girl," Mason said.

I frowned but tried to stay positive. "Well, I'll be here if you change your mind."

Mason narrowed his eyes. "Why are you nice to me?" he asked.

"Because there are always two sides to a story, and I don't know yours," I replied.

Mason was quiet. "You're different," he finally said. "I guess you're not that bad."

Was that his way of being nice?

Mason sat down near us and started telling jokes. At first, Joy and I didn't know what to do. But he was funny, and we began to laugh.

Abuelita was right—kindness was the only way to treat people.

Mama and Abuelita were waiting for me when the bus got to my stop. I said goodbye to Joy and Mason and walked down the steps.

Mama and Abuelita each gave me a big hug. I was glad to be home!

"How was school, Lola?" Abuelita asked.

"Better!" I said with a smile.

"How was it taking the bus both ways?" Mama asked. "Did that boy bother you again?"

I nodded. "But I was kind to him, just like you said, Abuelita. And it worked!"

Abuelita smiled at me. "Kindness can change the world!"

Chapter 8

All About You

Things were starting to feel normal at my new school. I still missed my old friends, but I liked my new ones too. And the bus wasn't scary anymore.

At recess, I hung out with Joy and Sophia. We went to our secret garden to continue building. Mud, rocks, and flowers were all that we needed to be happy.

Mrs. Bird told us to work with a partner during math class. I was glad Sophia was with me. I was really starting to like my new school!

But things changed that afternoon. Mrs. Bird reminded me about speaking to the class.

"We are excited you are here and can't wait to hear all about you!" Mrs. Bird said. "Do you think you'll be ready to talk to the class tomorrow?"

I sighed. I was never going to be ready, but I nodded.

I had been brave on the bus. I could be brave for this too.

When I got home that afternoon, I told Mama about talking to the class.

"Maybe it would help to write something down," she suggested.

I sat in the kitchen with a blank piece of paper. I grabbed a pencil and tried to write, but I couldn't come up with the right words.

What should I tell my class? I wondered.

After a while, Mama came in. She saw my blank paper.

"What's the problem?" she asked.

"I don't know what to write!" I was a little frustrated.

"You can talk about your family," Mama said. "Or tell them about your favorite color and your favorite food."

Those were all good ideas. I went to explore around the house to get some more inspiration.

When I walked past Mariana's nursery, Abuelita was in there rocking her. That gave me a great idea!

I ran to the kitchen and started writing. I finished in no time!

"Can I see it?" Abuelita asked when I was done.

"It's a surprise!" I told her.

After dinner, I went to say goodnight to Abuelita.

"¡Buenas noches!" she replied and gave me a big hug.

I went to my room and climbed into bed. A moment later, Mama came in. We said our prayers.

"¡Noches!" Mama said.

"Night!" I blew kisses. I couldn't wait to tell my class all about myself tomorrow!

Chapter 9

Breathe

In the morning, I got ready. I was starting to get used to my uniform. It was nice not having to think about what to wear each morning.

Abuelita was in the kitchen preparing my breakfast. "Ready for today?" she asked.

I nodded. "I think so. I just hope I don't get nervous talking in front of the class."

Abuelita gave me a hug. "Just imagine you are talking to me. You'll do great!"

When I got to my classroom, Mrs. Bird made an announcement right away.

"Today, Lola is going to tell us about herself," she said. "Everyone, please pay attention. Let's hear what she has to say."

I smiled nervously. *Be brave*, I told myself.

I went to the front of the class. My legs were shaking, and my hands were sweating. I made myself take a deep breath.

"Hi, everyone," I started. "My name is Lola. As you know, I'm new to the school."

Everyone stared at me. My heart started pounding. I forgot what I was saying.

"You are doing great, Lola!" Mrs. Bird said.

I closed my eyes for a second. I imagined Abuelita standing in front of me. I pictured myself talking to her. I was going to be okay.

"I live with my parents and with my little sister, Mariana," I continued. "The rest of my family lives in Guatemala. It is a small country below Mexico. It is about the size of Tennessee. It has a lot of volcanoes."

People seemed impressed by that, so I kept talking.

"When I grow up, I want to be an archaeologist." I said. "That's like an explorer. I will explore all the ancient Maya ruins my abuelita is always telling me about."

"What's an abuelita?" someone asked.

I smiled. "Abuelita is my grandmother. She is magical! She lives in Guatemala too, but she visits us once or twice a year. Abuelita is always nice and kind to everyone. I hope to be like her when I grow up."

"What's your favorite food?" someone asked from the back of the room.

I smiled. "My favorite food is whatever Abuelita cooks!"

"That's not a type of food!" one of my classmates said.

Something inside gave me courage, and I replied, "Guatemalan food is my favorite! I love refried beans and tamales. I wish you could all come to my house and try my abuelita's food!"

"Field trip!" hollered one of the boys.

"Great job, Lola!" Mrs. Bird said.

Sophia smiled at me. I smiled back. I had done it! I was not scared to speak in public anymore. Change was not that bad after all.

Chapter 10

Anything Is Possible

I had a giant smile on my face when I got off the bus that afternoon. I was happy.

"See you tomorrow!" I called to my friends on the bus.

Mama and Abuelita were waiting for me. "How was your day?" Mama asked.

"Great!" I replied. "I told everyone all about myself and my family and Guatemala."

"I can't believe how much you have grown, my sweet Lola!" said Mama.

I giggled at that. "What are you talking about, Mama?" I replied. "I'm the same height as before."

"You are not taller, but you are more confident. You are learning to make new friends and be brave!" said Mama proudly.

"That's because I learned something important," I said. "If you give things a chance, anything is possible!"

Abuelita smiled at me. "You seem happy!" she said. "Now, will you tell me what you wrote?"

"I told my class that you are magical," I said with a smile. "And that I want to be like you when I grow up!"

"You are so sweet, Lola. I love you!" Abuelita said.

"Thanks for all your advice!" I said.

I hugged Abuelita. Then, I hugged Mama. I could see Abuelita's joy in her eyes.

"Thank you for always believing in me. At first, I didn't want to change schools. It seemed scary. But now I am happy with my new friends!" I said.

"Sometimes change is what you need to see how strong you are, mija!" Mama told me.

I smiled proudly. I couldn't wait for the next day at my new school!

GLOSSARY

archaeologist (ar-kee-OLL-uh-jist)—a person who learns about the past by digging up old buildings or objects and studying them

chaos (KAY-os)—total confusion

confident (KON-fih-duhnt)—sure of oneself

contagious (kun-TAY-juss)—easy to spread

digestion (dye-JESS-chuhn)—the process a body uses to turn food into energy

legend (LEJ-uhnd)—a story handed down from earlier times; legends are often based on fact, but they are not entirely true

Maya (MY-uh)—a culture and ancient civilization stretching across southeastern Mexico and Central America, including Guatemala

rosary (ROH-zuh-ree)—a set of prayers used in the Catholic Church

ruins (ROO-ins)—the remains of a building or other things that have fallen down or been destroyed

sincere (sin-SEER)—being honest or true

tamales (tuh-MAH-less)—a Latin American food made of seasoned chicken or pork rolled in cornmeal, wrapped in banana leaves or corn husks, and steamed

uniform (YOO-nuh-form)—a special outfit that members of a particular group wear

SPANISH GLOSSARY

abuelita (aab-way-LEE-tah)—grandmother

buenas noches (BWEH-nahs NOH-ches)—good night

canillitas de leche (KAH-neh-YEE-tahs dey LEH-chay)—delicious treats made with powdered sugar and milk

colocho (koh-LOH-choh)—round, guava paste candy covered in sugar

hola (OH-lah)—hi or hello

La Llorona (lah yoh-ROH-nah)—a legendary figure believed to appear at night (near creeks or bodies of water) and cry for her children

mija (MEE-ha)—Spanish for "my daughter" but can also be used as a term of affection meaning "my child," "dear," or "honey"

Santo Cielo (SAHN-toh SYEH-loh)—an exclamation meaning "my goodness"

el Sombrerón (ehl sohm-breh-ROHN)—a legendary figure who is short, wears a big hat, and is believed to only appear at night

te amo (teh AH-moh)—I love you

TALK ABOUT IT

I. What three new students did Lola meet on her first day? What did she think about each of them at first, and how did her feelings change?

2. Look back through the story and identify some of Lola's favorite foods. Then think about your own favorite foods. What makes them your favorite?

3. On her first day at her new school, Lola wears red bows, which help her stand out. Are there things you like to wear or do that make you unique?

WRITE IT DOWN

1. Lola is worried about being the new kid. Have you ever been to a new place or in a new situation? Write a list of ideas for things you can do to cope when you're feeling worried.

2. Abuelita tells Lola that there are two sides to every story. Have you ever had an argument? Write a paragraph about what happened. What was the other person's side? How did you solve it?

3. Lola learns that something as simple as a smile can brighten someone's day. Make a list of other small acts of kindness. (For example: picking up your dishes after eating, throwing out your trash, telling someone thank you, or just smiling!)

ABUELITA'S FRESHLY SQUEEZED LIMEADE

Did you know that in Spanish, the words for lemons and limes are reversed? In Spanish, the green fruit is a limón (lemon), and the yellow fruit is a lima (lime). So when you ask for lemonade (limonada) in Spanish, you are actually getting limeade. That's why Abuelita's limeade is yellow instead of green!

WHAT YOU NEED

- a large pitcher
- 16 cups water
- 5 tablespoons sugar
- a big spoon
- 5 limes
- a sharp knife
- a strainer

WHAT TO DO

1. Pour the sugar and water into the pitcher. Stir until the sugar is dissolved.

2. Cut the limes in half. (Be safe—make sure to have an adult do the cutting!)

3. Place the strainer on top of the pitcher. Squeeze the limes through the strainer.

4. Remove the strainer. Use the spoon to give the mixture another stir.

5. Serve! (You can add ice, but remember, Abuelita thinks it tastes better without!)

ABOUT THE AUTHOR

Keka Novales grew up in Guatemala City, Guatemala, which is located in Central America. Growing up, she wanted to be a doctor, a vet, a ballerina, an engineer, and a writer. Keka moved several times and changed schools, so she has plenty of experience being the "new kid." Her grandparents had a vital role in her life. Abuelo was always making jokes, and Abuelita helped everyone around her. Keka currently lives with her family in Denton, Texas.

Photo credit JCPenney

ABOUT THE ILLUSTRATOR

Gloria Félix was born and raised in Uruapan, a beautiful, small city in Michoacán, Mexico. Her home is one of her biggest inspirations when it comes to art. Her favorite things to do growing up were drawing, watching cartoons, and eating, which are still some of her favorite things to do. Gloria currently lives and paints in Los Angeles, California.

Photo credit Gloria Félix